This Book Belongs To:

_____

Adapted from the original "Twelve Days of Christmas" holiday carol.

For information regarding permission write:
Books to Bed, Inc.
224 West 35th Street, Room 700, New York, NY.10001

Library of Congress Cataloging-in-Publication Data on file
ISBN 978-1-4507-2478-4

First Edition-7th Printing

Printed in China

Visit www.Bookstobed.com

12
DAYS OF
CHRISTMAS

Adapted By

Books to Bed

Illustrated By
Tory Novikova

ORIGINAL
12 Days of Christmas

On the first day of Christmas,
My true love sent to me
A partridge in a pear tree.

On the second day of Christmas,
My true love sent to me
Two turtle doves,

On the third day of Christmas,
My true love sent to me
Three French hens,

On the fourth day of Christmas,
My true love sent to me
Four calling birds,

On the fifth day of Christmas,
My true love sent to me
Five golden rings,

On the sixth day of Christmas,
My true love sent to me
Six geese a-laying,

On the seventh day of Christmas,
My true love sent to me
Seven swans a-swimming,

On the eighth day of Christmas,
My true love sent to me
Eight maids a-milking,

On the ninth day of Christmas,
My true love sent to me
Nine ladies dancing,

On the tenth day of Christmas,
My true love sent to me
Ten lords a-leaping,

On the eleventh day of Christmas,
My true love sent to me
Eleven pipers piping,

On the twelfth day of Christmas,
My true love sent to me
Twelve drummers drumming,
Eleven pipers piping,
Ten lords a-leaping,
Nine ladies dancing,
Eight maids a-milking,
Seven swans a-swimming,
Six geese a-laying,
Five golden rings,
Four calling birds,
Three French hens,
Two turtle doves,
And a partridge in a pear tree!

On the first day of Christmas,
it was my delight to see...

A package my loved ones sent me!

FROM:
Grandma
&
Grandpa

On the second day of Christmas,
it was my delight to see...

Two Transforming Robots
From a package my uncle sent me!

On the third day of Christmas, it was my delight to see...

Three Fairy Princesses
Two Transforming Robots
From a package my auntie sent me!

On the fourth day of Christmas,
it was my delight to see...

Four Choo-choo Trains
Three Fairy Princesses
Two Transforming Robots
From a package my dad sent me!

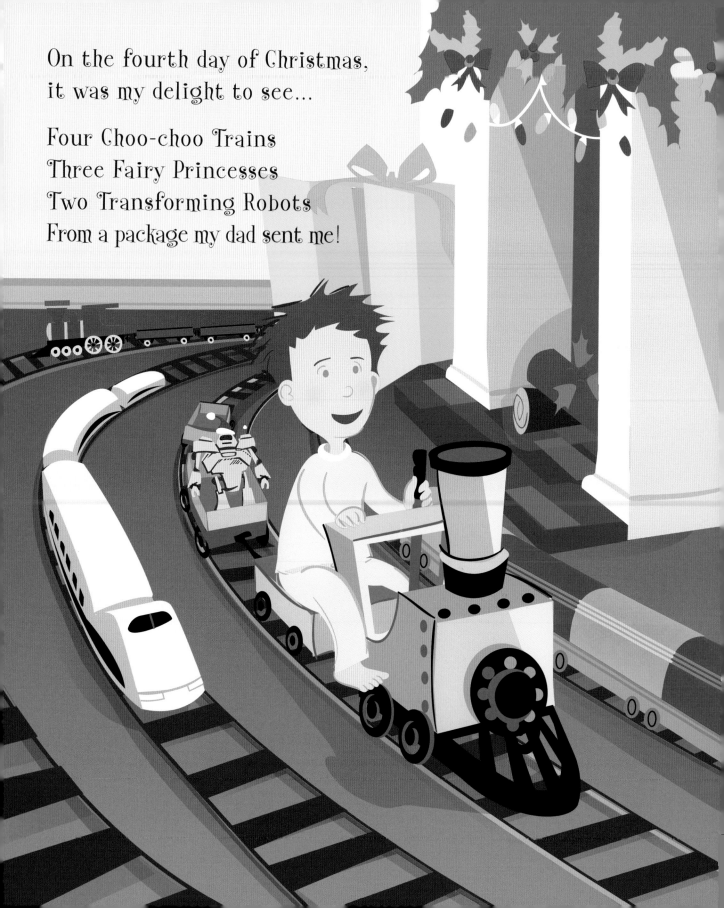

On the fifth day of Christmas, it was my delight to see...

Five Golden Things
Four Choo-choo Trains
Three Fairy Princesses
Two Transforming Robots
From a package my mom sent me!

On the sixth day of Christmas, it was my delight to see...

Six Scooters a-Scooting,
Five Golden Things
Four Choo-choo Trains
Three Fairy Princesses
Two Transforming Robots
From a package my brother sent me!

On the seventh day of Christmas,
it was my delight to see...

Seven Kittens Purring
Six Scooters a-Scooting
Five Golden Things
Four Choo-choo Trains
Three Fairy Princesses
Two Transforming Robots
From a package my sister sent me!

On the eighth day of Christmas,
it was my delight to see...

Eight Sneakers a-Wheeling
Seven Kittens Purring
Six Scooters a-Scooting
Five Golden Things
Four Choo-choo Trains
Three Fairy Princesses
Two Transforming Robots
From a package my cousin sent me!

On the nineth day of Christmas,
it was my delight to see...

Nine Ballerinas a-Twirling
Eight Sneakers a-Wheeling
Seven Kittens Purring
Six Scooters a-Scooting
Five Golden Things
Four Choo-choo Trains
Three Fairy Princesses
Two Transforming Robots
From a package my friend sent me!

On the tenth day of Christmas,
it was my delight to see...

Ten Guitars a-Playing
Nine Ballerinas a-Twirling
Eight Sneakers a-Wheeling
Seven Kittens Purring
Six Scooters a-Scooting
Five Golden Things
Four Choo choo Trains
Three Fairy Princesses
Two Transforming Robots
From a package my teacher sent me!

On the eleventh day of Christmas, it was my delight to see...

Eleven Dinosaurs a-Roaring
Ten Guitars a-Playing
Nine Ballerinas a-Twirling
Eight Sneakers a-Wheeling
Seven Kittens Purring
Six Scooters a-Scooting

Five Golden Things
Four Choo-choo Trains
Three Fairy Princesses
Two Transforming Robots
From a package my classmate sent me!

On the twelfth day of Christmas,
it was my delight to see...

Twelve Cameras Flashing
Eleven Dinosaurs a-Roaring
Ten Guitars a-Playing
Nine Ballerinas a-Twirling
Eight Sneakers a-Wheeling
Seven Kittens Purring
Six Scooters a-Scooting
Five Golden Things
Four Choo-choo Trains
Three Fairy Princesses
Two Transforming Robots
From a package my loved ones sent me!

Books to Bed Publications

In a faraway place named Neverland
lived a magical boy they called Peter Pan.
Come soar through the sky on a fantastic trip
with mermaids, adventure and Hook's pirate ship!
This timeless story of Pan and his friends
will captivate children from beginning to end!

Retold in Rhyme by Ilene Bauer & Jill Cozza-Turner
Illustrated by Alisa Grodsky

Cinderella was sweet, but sad as could be,
from her selfish stepsisters she wanted to flee.
Join her on a journey of hope and true love
and a tiny glass slipper that fits like a glove.
This classic tale is a helpful reminder, that
"good things will come if you treat others kinder."

Retold in Rhyme by Ilene Bauer
Illustrated by Tory Novikova

"Twas the Night Before Christmas" is a timeless classic that families have shared and loved for nearly 180 years. This heartwarming tale with wonderful images of Santa and his reindeer continues to provide opportunities for families to red together and create holiday traditions both parents and children will remember and enjoy.

Poem by Clement C. Moore
Illustrated by Alisa Grodsky

"Casey at Bat" is a poem about baseball written in 1888 by Ernest Thayer. In our illustrated version, the excitement of the crowd is personified in our young fan commenting on the game, caught up in the drama of the team's star player striking out. Have fun filling out baseball trivia and brain teasers inside the book!

Adapted by Jill Cozza-Turner
Illustrated by Alisa Grodsky

12 DAYS OF CHRISTMAS

TRAINS A-WHISTLING

SNEAKERS A-WHEELING

On the 2nd
Day of
Chris...

On the 3rd
Day of
Christmas